STAR WARS
THE LAST JEDI
WARS ™

ADAPTED BY ELIZABETH SCHAEFER

ILLUSTRATIONS BY BRIAN ROOD

BASED ON THE SCREENPLAY BY RIAN JOHNSON

DISNEY
LUCASFILM
PRESS

LOS ANGELES · NEW YORK

Printed in the United States of America

First Hardcover Edition, March 2018

1 3 5 7 9 10 8 6 4 2

Library of Congress Control Number on file

FAC-038091-18019

ISBN 978-1-4847-0556-8

Visit the official *Star Wars* website at: www.starwars.com.

SUSTAINABLE FORESTRY INITIATIVE

Certified Sourcing

www.sfiprogram.org

SFI-00993

Logo Applies to Text Stock Only

The FIRST ORDER reigns. Having decimated the peaceful Republic, Supreme Leader Snoke now deploys his merciless legions to seize military control of the galaxy.

Only General Leia Organa's small band of RESISTANCE fighters stand against the rising tyranny, certain that Jedi Master Luke Skywalker will return and restore a spark of hope to the fight.

But the Resistance has been exposed. As the First Order speeds toward the rebel base, the brave heroes mount a desperate escape. . . .

GENERAL LEIA ORGANA SHOUTED OUT ORDERS

as Resistance fighters scrambled to gather supplies. Their daring attack against the First Order's Starkiller Base had crippled Supreme Leader Snoke's evil army. But the attack had also exposed the Resistance's location to its enemy. Now Leia and her soldiers had to leave D'Qar—and fast!

Leia knew the Resistance transports needed more time to safely reach the rest of the fleet in space. She turned to her best pilot, Poe Dameron, for help. She could already see a glint of mischief in his eyes.

"You've got an idea," she said. "But I won't like it."

Poe opened his mouth to explain, but Leia knew every second mattered.

"Go," she said.

General Hux surveyed the destruction of D'Qar from the bridge of a First Order Star Destroyer.

"We've caught them in the middle of their evacuation," a First Order officer explained.

"Perfect," Hux said. "Snuff out the Resistance once and for all."

But then Hux heard something surprising.

"Attention, this is Commander Poe Dameron of the Republic fleet. I have an urgent communiqué for General Hugs."

Poe was actually *communicating* with the First Order as he and his droid, BB-8, flew toward the evil army's fleet in his black X-wing. There was no way the small starfighter could fight so many ships alone, but Poe had a plan.

"This is General *Hux* of the First Order," Hux clarified. "Your fleet are rebel scum and war criminals. Tell your precious princess there will be no terms. There will be no surrender."

Poe kept Hux talking and distracted until his X-wing's booster rocket was fully charged, then he sped toward the deadly First Order Dreadnought! By that point, he was too close to the ship for it to fire at him.

Poe cut off his conversation with Hux and began taking out the Dreadnought's powerful surface cannons. His plan had worked!

With most of the Dreadnought's cannons destroyed, Resistance A-wings, X-wings, and heavy bombers joined the battle.

"Bombers, keep that formation tight," the lead bomber pilot ordered. "Let's do some damage and buy our fleet some time."

Poe just needed to take out the Dreadnought's final working artillery.
"One cannon left . . ." Poe said as he lined up his shot.
But before he could fire, an enemy blast hit his weapons systems.

BB-8 ducked into the hull of the starfighter and began repairing the damaged wires as quickly as he could.

A squadron of TIE fighters was swarming Poe's disabled ship.

BB-8 repaired the X-wing's weapons systems just in time!

Poe's attack run had allowed all the Resistance transports to make it to safety.

"Poe, you did it," Leia said over the comm. "Now get your squad back here."

Poe hesitated. "No. We can finish this!"

Poe wanted to destroy the Dreadnought once and for all, so he led the Resistance bombers on a dangerous attack run.

So many of the heavy Resistance ships were destroyed in the battle that, finally, there was only one bomber left.

Inside that bomber, a young gunner named Paige prepared to drop its bombs on the Dreadnought. But the remote to release the bombs teetered high above her on a ladder.

Paige had been hurt from an explosion and could not climb the ladder, but she hammered on the metal frame from down below, desperately trying to get the remote to fall down to where she was. Without her bombs, the Dreadnought would still be operational.

"Now! Drop it now!" Poe ordered Paige's bomber.

Paige kicked the ladder one last time with all her strength, and the remote finally fell down, right into her hand. She pressed a red button on the remote and the bombs dropped onto the Dreadnought.

The massive First Order ship shuddered under the blast of the bombs and exploded in a burst of light and heat.

Paige closed her eyes as her ship plummeted toward the exploding Dreadnought. It was too late for the bomber to escape, but Paige knew her sacrifice would keep the Resistance safe.

The Dreadnought had been destroyed.
It was time for Poe and what remained of his crew of fighters to return to the main Resistance cruiser so they could jump to hyperspace and escape the First Order.

As the Resistance fleet jumped to the safety of hyperspace, former First Order stormtrooper Finn woke with a start inside a medbay on the main Resistance cruiser. He was wearing a strange healing bacta suit.

Finn had been badly hurt during the battle on Starkiller Base. The last thing he remembered was fighting the evil First Order warrior Kylo Ren to protect his friend Rey.

What had happened after that?

As he shuffled through the ship searching for answers, Finn was relieved to see his friend Poe.

"Buddy!" Poe said. "Let's get you dressed. You must have a thousand questions."

But Finn had only one.

"Where's Rey?"

At that moment, Rey was far, far away, racing across the galaxy in the *Millennium Falcon* with her Wookiee copilot, Chewbacca, and the faithful droid R2-D2.

General Leia had sent Rey on a mission.

Rey and Leia knew that the power of the First Order could not be undone with ships and weapons alone. While the strength of General Hux's fleet was terrifying, the true might of the First Order lay with Supreme Leader Snoke and his apprentice, Kylo Ren, Leia's own son, once known as Ben Solo. The two warriors used the dark side of the Force to destroy anyone who challenged them.

Only a Jedi could stand up to their power. And Leia's brother, Luke Skywalker, was the last Jedi.

So Leia had sent Rey to find Luke.

The *Falcon* landed on a craggy island on the remote planet of Ahch-To.

It was rumored that the first Jedi temple was located on the ancient planet, and Rey could feel that the Force had a powerful presence on the island.

She was searching for Luke, and she had found him.

The Jedi removed his hood as Rey approached. She offered Luke his old lightsaber. It had seen her through her first battle with Kylo Ren, back on the First Order's Starkiller Base, after he had hurt her friend Finn.

But when Luke finally took the lightsaber from Rey, he tossed it carelessly behind him and walked away.

Rey was shocked.

"Master Skywalker?" she called after him, confused by what had just happened.

Rey followed Luke around the edge of a cliff and back to a small hut on top of a jagged slope.

"I'm from the Resistance. General Leia sent me," she explained. "We need you to come back."

But Luke refused to listen. Instead, he slammed the door in Rey's face.

Rey had no idea what to do.
Why wouldn't Luke talk to her?
Rey went to retrieve the lightsaber.
She found it on a grassy ledge, high
above what looked like an old X-wing,
sunken beneath the waves.

It seemed as though Luke had no
intention of ever leaving the island.

If Luke wouldn't listen to her, Rey thought he might pay attention to an old friend. So Rey brought Chewbacca to Luke's hut.

Chewie burst through the door, howling loudly.

Luke was surprised to see his old friend.

"Chewie. What are you doing here?"

Luke couldn't ignore the weight of history between them.

"Long story," Rey said, starting to feel some hope. "We'll tell you on the *Falcon*."

"The *Falcon*?" Luke asked. For the first time, a shiver of emotion crossed his face as he thought of his past life, flying in the old ship with his friends.

"Where's Han?" he asked—though he feared he already knew the answer.

Han Solo was gone. He had tried to save his and Leia's son back on the First Order's Starkiller Base, even though Snoke had turned their Ben Solo into the evil Kylo Ren.

But Han and Leia's son had returned Han's love with betrayal. Kylo had ended his father's life. He had not been able to defeat the young Force-sensitive Rey though—and Snoke was displeased.

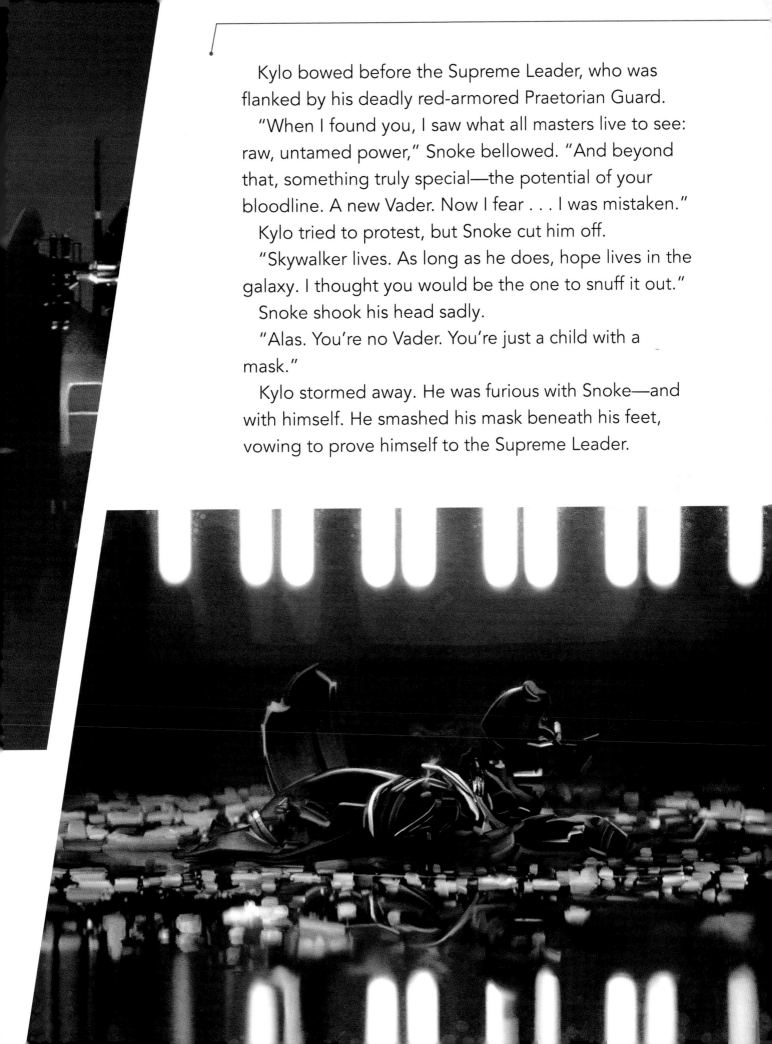

Kylo bowed before the Supreme Leader, who was flanked by his deadly red-armored Praetorian Guard.

"When I found you, I saw what all masters live to see: raw, untamed power," Snoke bellowed. "And beyond that, something truly special—the potential of your bloodline. A new Vader. Now I fear . . . I was mistaken."

Kylo tried to protest, but Snoke cut him off.

"Skywalker lives. As long as he does, hope lives in the galaxy. I thought you would be the one to snuff it out."

Snoke shook his head sadly.

"Alas. You're no Vader. You're just a child with a mask."

Kylo stormed away. He was furious with Snoke—and with himself. He smashed his mask beneath his feet, vowing to prove himself to the Supreme Leader.

Back on the Resistance cruiser, Leia was furious with Poe. He had deliberately disobeyed her orders.

"You're demoted," she told Poe.

He would now be a captain instead of a commander.

"For what?" the pilot protested. "We took out a Dreadnought!"

Leia held Poe's gaze, letting him carefully consider her words.

"There are things you can't solve by jumping in an X-wing and blowing something up. I need you to learn that."

"There were heroes on that mission," Poe insisted.

"Dead heroes," Leia said. "No leaders."

Silence hung in the air, only to be broken by the blare of alarms.

"Proximity alert!" Admiral Ackbar shouted.

Through the viewport, Poe, Leia, and Ackbar saw the First Order fleet burst out of hyperspace.

Thirty Star Destroyers emerged from hyperspace, flanked by Snoke's Mega-Destroyer. They loomed over the small Resistance fleet.

How could the First Order have tracked the Resistance through hyperspace? The Resistance couldn't fight such a massive array of ships. And they had only enough fuel for one more lightspeed jump. But there was no point in wasting that fuel if the First Order could track them through hyperspace.

The Resistance's only hope was to save fuel and fly as fast as it could at sublight speed away from the First Order. But the enemy was already launching TIE fighters, ready to attack.

Poe needed to do something to help. He turned to Leia.

"Permission to jump in an X-wing and blow something up?"

Leia nodded.

Poe ran toward the hangar bay and prepared to jump in his X-wing and defend the Resistance fleet.

"Don't wait for me!" Poe called out to BB-8, who rolled ahead of him at top speed. "Jump in and fire her up!"

Kylo raced toward the main Resistance cruiser in his deadly TIE silencer. He was ready to prove himself to Snoke.

Flying deep inside the Resistance ship, the black walls of his prototype TIE silencer were nearly invisible to his enemies' sensors.

Without warning, Kylo burst into the hangar and opened fire.

Poe had almost reached his X-wing when Kylo's blast burned through the bay. Poe covered his eyes as flames surrounded his ship. Half the hangar was destroyed, including Poe's X-wing and many other starfighters. Their only hope now was to move the fleet out of range of the Star Destroyers.

With the hangar ruined, Kylo focused his weapons on the command bridge.

Stretching out with the Force, Kylo sensed his mother, General Leia, on board the ship. At last, he would be able to destroy his past once and for all.

But as he sensed Leia's presence, he was surprised to feel her sensing his. He anticipated a wave of hatred and anger. But instead he felt only love and . . . sadness.

Kylo shook off the connection. He needed to finish what he had started back on Starkiller Base.

He placed his finger on the trigger, but hesitated. Could he really destroy his own mother?

The question went
unanswered as a fellow TIE
fighter fired and destroyed
the bridge. Kylo saw the still
form of his mother as she
was sucked out into space.

Just then, Hux's voice
sounded over Kylo's comm.

"The Resistance have
pulled out of range. Return
to the fleet," he ordered.

Kylo pounded his console in frustration. At the most important moment,
Kylo had failed, just as Snoke had told him he would. But as Kylo returned to
his fleet, he still sensed Leia's presence.

Lost in the darkness of space, Leia had refused to give up. With her last bit
of strength, she reached out with the Force and pulled herself back into the
safety of her ship.

After Rey had told Luke about Han's death and Kylo's betrayal, she hoped he would understand why the Resistance needed him. But Luke still refused to join her. So Rey followed him around Ahch-To, pleading with the Jedi to change his mind. She refused to give up.

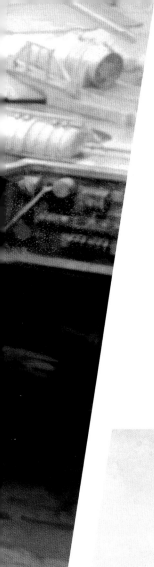

Luke scurried from place to place, doing his daily chores—fishing for food and collecting milk from a large sea cow—but not once did he look back at Rey.

Then, as Rey followed Luke past a hollow tree, she stopped.

Rey had only just begun to understand the call of the Force, to open herself to its power and instructions. But she knew immediately that this cave was more than what it seemed.

She turned from Luke and headed toward the tree.

For the first time, Luke stopped, too. How had Rey been able to sense the tree's power?

Luke followed Rey into the darkened chamber and watched as she made her way toward a mossy cleft in the tree. She followed the pull of the Force to a shelf where six dusty books were waiting for her. As she reached out to touch them, the very air around them seemed to shimmer.

"Who are you?" Luke breathed.

Now Rey had his attention.

"Where are you from?" he asked.

"Nowhere," said Rey.

"No one's from nowhere," the Jedi countered.

"Jakku," Rey confessed.

Luke raised an eyebrow. "All right, that is pretty much nowhere. Why are you here, Rey from nowhere?"

"Something inside me has always been there, but now it's awake and . . . I'm afraid," Rey said.

Luke understood. "You want a teacher."

Rey nodded.

"I can't teach you," Luke said sadly. He had tried to train his nephew, Ben Solo, to be a Jedi. But then Ben had turned to the dark side and become the evil Kylo Ren, and Luke blamed himself.

"It's time for the Jedi to end."

Back on the main Resistance cruiser, Leia was confined to the medbay. She had survived the First Order's attack, but she was unable to lead her fleet. Finn knew the Resistance was in trouble, but he didn't know what to do.

Then BB-8 showed Finn a holorecording from when Rey said good-bye to him while he was in the medbay, before she left for Ahch-To. Suddenly, Finn knew exactly what to do. He would go find his friend and help her.

Finn planned to steal an escape pod, but as he was boarding one, a technician named Rose spotted him.

"You're Finn!" she said with a huge smile.

Rose was thrilled to meet a hero from the Resistance's battle on Starkiller Base—that was, until she realized Finn was planning to run away.

Finn tried to explain. "Listen . . ."

Rose would *not* listen. Her sister, Paige, had sacrificed herself for the Resistance during the recent battle with the First Order. And now this traitor wanted to abandon the cause Paige had given her life for? Rose pulled out a small electro-stun prod and zapped Finn unconscious.

With General Leia unable to lead and the First Order in pursuit, the Resistance needed a plan of action. Fortunately, Leia had left clear instructions for her trusted friend Vice Admiral Holdo to take command if anything were to happen to her.

But Holdo and Poe had very different ideas about how to fight the First Order.

"We need to shake them before we find another base," Poe insisted. "What's our plan?"

"*Captain* Dameron, that is need-to-know information, and you do not need to know," Holdo explained, using Poe's demoted rank. "Stick to your post and follow my orders."

Rey wasn't making much progress with Luke back on Ahch-To, either. Frustrated with the elusive Jedi, Rey went to train while Chewie spent time with the little porgs that lived on the island.

Chewie had been annoyed by the small birdlike creatures at first. But the Wookiee had started to warm up to them.

While Chewie made new friends, Luke found an old friend on board the *Millennium Falcon*.

"Artoo?" Luke asked.

The droid rolled forward and buzzed angrily at his former master. His meaning was clear: the Resistance needed a Jedi.

"Old friend, I'm doing what's best," Luke said. "Nothing can change my mind.

In answer, R2 projected a familiar hologram.

A blue-tinged image of young Leia spoke to him: "You're my only hope."

Luke was caught off guard by the hologram that had started his adventures years and years before. What would have happened to the galaxy if he had ignored Leia then as he was doing now?

A sliver of doubt entered Luke's mind.

He found Rey sleeping in front of his hut.

Waking her up, Luke said, "Tomorrow. At dawn. I will teach you the ways of the Jedi. And why they need to end."

Across the galaxy, Rose's electro-stun had worn off and Finn was pleading with her to let him go. He explained that now that the First Order could track them through hyperspace, the Resistance was doomed. Rose turned this new information over in her mind. Instead of being afraid, she was excited. Rose realized that the First Order must be tracking them from a single ship, the Mega-Destroyer. If they could sneak on to that ship, she could shut down the tracker.

Finn hated to admit it, but he was the perfect person to get her there. As a former stormtrooper, he knew First Order ships inside and out. And if they could stop the First Order, he could go and find Rey. . . .

Finn and Rose told Poe their plan. It was risky, but Poe liked risky ideas. And Vice Admiral Holdo hadn't done a thing since she had taken charge of the Resistance. Poe knew it was up to him and his friends to save the fleet.

The only problem was that Rose and Finn would need clearance codes to board the Mega-Destroyer. Fortunately, their old friend Maz Kanata knew just the person to help them: the Master Codebreaker, last seen in the lavish city of Canto Bight on Cantonica.

Poe helped Rose, Finn, and BB-8 sneak away in a ship, and soon the unlikely trio was traveling to Canto Bight to find the Master Codebreaker.

Back on Ahch-To, Rey tossed and turned in her sleep.

When she opened her eyes, she was shocked to see Kylo Ren seated across the room.

Without hesitating, Rey grabbed her blaster and fired at the dark warrior who had hurt so many people she cared about. But the blast passed right through him.

Rey didn't understand what was going on, but she was certain this was no dream. Even though they were light-years apart, the two were connected through the Force.

The door behind Rey opened and Kylo vanished. Luke had arrived to begin Rey's training, and he looked quizzically at the smoking blaster hole in the hut wall.

Rey quickly lied, telling him that her blaster had accidentally fired while she was cleaning it.

As she followed Luke out of the hut, she knew she should tell him about her strange vision, but something held her back. If Luke kept secrets, so could she.

Luke's first goal was to show Rey how to open up to the Force and how to protect herself from the dark side. He took her to a ledge and showed her how to meditate.

Rey felt the Force pulsing around her, as if the answer to any question might be found just outside her grasp. If she could only . . .

The ground began to shake around them.

"This place can show me something." Rey grew excited. Finally, she might learn the secrets of her past. The ground quaked even more as Rey concentrated harder, until finally Luke broke her out of her trance.

"You went straight to the dark." Luke shook his head. "It offered you something you needed, and you didn't even try to stop yourself."

Rey realized Luke looked more afraid than angry.

"I've seen this raw strength only once before . . . in Ben Solo."

Rey continued her training with Luke, but her Force connections with Kylo continued, too. They even started speaking to each other.

While Rey was suspicious of the dark First Order warrior, she also sensed conflict in him. She began to hope that he might be brought back to the light side of the Force.

But Kylo had his own agenda. He knew Luke was keeping secrets from Rey.

"Has he told you what happened? The night I destroyed his temple?" Kylo asked, staring intently at Rey. "Has he told you why?"

Meanwhile, Rose, Finn, and BB-8 had arrived in the beautiful, glittering city of Canto Bight to find the Master Codebreaker.

There the rich and powerful hid from the conflict in the galaxy. Many of them even made their fortunes by selling weapons to fighters on both sides of the war. They didn't care how many people died, as long as the fighting continued and the credits kept rolling in.

As Finn, Rose, and BB-8 entered one of the casinos, Finn was impressed by the glitz and glamour that surrounded them. He had never seen such wealth and opulence in all his life. Everywhere he looked, humans and strange aliens decked out in the galaxy's finest enjoyed games of chance and rare delicacies.

But Rose was disgusted. It was those exact people who had sold weapons to the First Order—weapons that helped destroy her homeworld.

BB-8 didn't mind Canto Bight.
    One alien had mistaken the little droid for a game machine and kept giving him coins.
    BB-8 beeped and whirred like the nearby game machines, playing along to get more coins.

Rose noticed a beautiful window featuring images of the fathiers that were raced for sport on Canto Bight. The sight of the graceful animals filled Rose with joy and sadness. Fathiers had been Paige's favorite animal, even though she had never gotten to see a real one.

Thinking of Paige, Rose showed Finn the medallion on a cord around her neck—the medallion her sister had carried the other half of.

Finn recognized it as the symbol of the Otomok system.

"The First Order would raze our cities to test whatever weapons, steal our kids for recruitment," she said.

"I know," Finn said sadly. Finn had been one of the many children taken by the First Order from many different worlds. They were forced to serve as First Order soldiers.

Suddenly, BB-8 rolled up to Finn and Rose, rattling with coins. He had found the Master Codebreaker!

The Master Codebreaker was at one of the biggest, most expensive tables in the casino.

Maz had told them that he would help the Resistance. All Finn and Rose needed to do was introduce themselves and they would be one step closer to disabling the First Order tracking system and freeing the Resistance fleet!

On Ahch-To, Rey was one step closer to finding out the truth about Luke and Kylo, and why Luke wanted the Jedi to end.

Luke had taken Rey to the old Jedi temple for this important conversation.

"The legacy of the Jedi is failure," Luke said.

He told Rey what had happened with Kylo.

"By the time I realized I was no match for the darkness rising in him, it was too late."

Kylo had listened to Snoke's promises of power and destroyed Luke's training temple, leaving Luke for dead.

Luke blamed himself for not stopping Kylo. Now his former student threatened the galaxy. So Luke had cut himself off from the Force and sworn never to teach another student.

"You didn't fail Kylo—*he* failed *you*," Rey said. "I won't."

But Luke simply walked out of the temple, refusing to listen to Rey.

When Rey followed Luke outside, she saw six wooden ships headed toward them.

"It's a tribe from a neighboring island," Luke explained. "They come once a month to raid and plunder."

"We have to stop them!" Rey said.

She raced across the cliffs, leaping over rocks and pools of water, toward a cluster of huts to defend the helpless Caretakers who lived peacefully on the island.

But the "attackers" had not come to raid but to celebrate!

The Visitors were dancing and feasting with the Caretakers. Even Chewie and R2 had joined the fun.

Luke reached Rey's side. He leaned over, trying to catch his breath.

"I'm sorry, I didn't think you'd—you just ran so fast."

Rey was confused.

"I thought they were in danger," she said. "I was just trying to do something."

"And that's what the Resistance needs," Luke said.

He believed Rey already knew how to fight for justice. She didn't need old Jedi tricks.

"Do you understand now?" the Jedi asked.

Back on Canto Bight, the local police had gotten in the way of Finn and Rose's plan to ask the Master Codebreaker for help.

The Canto cops had found the small Resistance ship crashed on a beach and threw Finn and Rose in jail!

Canto Bight's jail was nothing like the beautiful city around it. Dark, grimy walls pressed in on Finn and Rose in their cell.

But Finn and Rose were not alone. In the corner of the cell hunched a disheveled man. He didn't even look up when they entered, but he soon grew tired of the pair arguing over what to do next. He interrupted their disagreement and introduced himself as DJ. Rose and Finn could tell that this was hardly his first time in prison.

DJ claimed he could escape at any time; the jail was just a quiet place to sleep.

Rose and Finn were skeptical of DJ's claim. Could he really break them out of the cell so easily? In response, DJ walked up to the heavy door and slid a card into the security panel. Within seconds, they were free.

Rose caught Finn's eye. She was thinking the same thing: they might have lost Maz's Master Codebreaker, but the galaxy seemed to have provided them with someone just as skilled. They had to convince DJ to help them.

Just then, the prison alarm began to sound. DJ waved and then ran to the exit, disappearing ahead of them.

Meanwhile, BB-8 was searching for his friends. He had followed them to the prison but entered just as the alarm began to sound. He had to think quickly if he was going to help Rose and Finn escape.

Then the little droid remembered all the coins the alien had given him. BB-8 fired the coins at the guards like missiles and then zapped them with his electro-prod. By the time BB-8 was done, the guards were tied up in a pile on the floor.

Finn and Rose became separated from DJ during their escape and they were hiding in the fathier stables near the prison.

Rose was in awe of the massive creatures.

But the building was not as empty as they had hoped. . . .

A young boy was feeding the racing fathiers inside. He was startled to see Rose and Finn and reached for an alarm.

But then the boy quickly took in their ordinary clothes and their kind faces. Clearly they didn't belong in Canto Bight. Rose explained that they had come to this planet to help save the galaxy.

"Are you with the Resistance?" the boy asked.

Rose raised a finger to her lips and nodded. Then she showed him a ring on her finger with a secret rebel insignia.

The boy's eyes grew wide, but he stayed silent. Rose smiled.

Rose and Finn checked the stable door and started to head back toward the spaceport, but they were spotted by a security patrol! There was no way they could outrun the officers on foot, but Finn had an idea. He leapt onto the back of a fathier and helped Rose climb on behind him while the boy opened the gates for the other fathiers to escape.

The fathier that Finn and Rose were riding galloped into the busy streets of Canto Bight. The stable boy had released the entire herd behind them, creating confusion and panic.

The fathiers tore through the casino and out into the beautiful city, trampling glamorous speeders and even crashing through one of the ballrooms!

The Canto Bight police had hopped on their speeders and were catching up with Rose and Finn and the herd.

The beasts ran to the edge of the city and away from the shining lights.

"*Cliff!*" Finn suddenly shouted.

Their fathier skidded to a halt.

There seemed to be no escape.

Then a bright spotlight shone down on them. It was the light from a sleek sports ship.

DJ and BB-8 had found a way to rescue them!

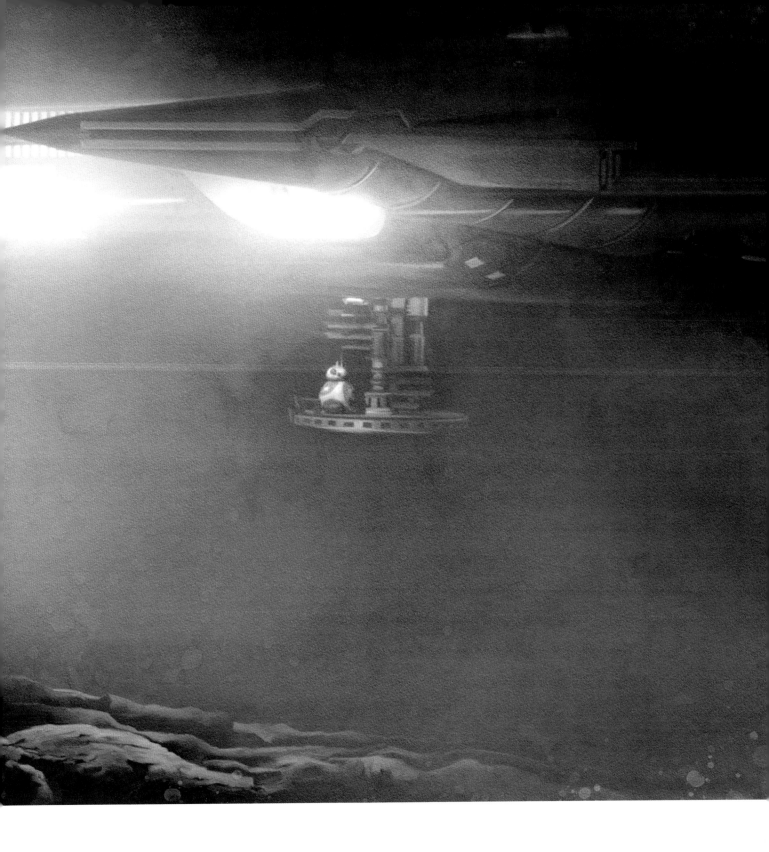

Rose and Finn jumped on board and watched as DJ piloted the ship into hyperspace.

They were safe. They just needed to convince DJ to help them with their mission to stop the First Order.

On Ahch-To, Rey and Kylo's Force connections had continued, and Kylo was trying to convince Rey that Luke hadn't told her the truth. Kylo said that Luke had tried to kill him, long before Snoke showed him his true path. Kylo claimed Luke was afraid of Kylo's power. Rather than try to train Kylo, Luke had simply tried to destroy him.

Rey knew Kylo had every reason to lie to her. And yet something about his words felt true. Rey needed to be alone, to clear her mind and listen to the Force.

As she walked, she felt the Force guiding her.

Suddenly, the ground gave way beneath Rey's feet. She fell into a gaping cave. The walls around her shone like black glass, reflecting her face.

It was as if the questions that constantly whispered in the back of Rey's mind were turned up to a roar. Why did Luke turn his back on his own student? Was there still good in Kylo? And what if that same darkness was inside Rey, too? Would Luke turn on her, as well?

These thoughts were soon drowned out by the biggest questions of all— the questions that had followed Rey her whole life. Who were her parents? Why had they abandoned her on Jakku? Did they know then that she could use the Force? Had they been afraid of her?

As Rey's fears multiplied, she seemed to see endless versions of herself in the cave walls—but none of the Reys held the answers she was looking for.

It took all Rey's strength to escape from the cave. But the questions still followed her. Without thinking, Rey raced back to her hut and reached out for comfort. She reached out to Kylo.

This time, Rey saw nothing but concern in the villain's eyes. She knew there was darkness inside her, but she also knew she could overcome it. And so could Kylo.

"It's not too late!" Rey told him.

She reached out to take his hand, and Kylo grasped her trembling fingers. Instantly, they were both overwhelmed with images of the future and the past.

Just then, Luke opened the door to Rey's hut and saw Rey and Kylo clasping hands. Luke was furious.

"Is it true? Did you try to murder him?" Rey asked.

"Leave now!" Luke shouted back. His raw connection to the Force swelled, exploding the hut around them. He regretted ever allowing Rey to stay on Ahch-To. He knew now that she would fall to darkness, just as Kylo had before her. Luke's cold anger frightened Rey, severing her connection with Kylo.

But Rey wasn't going to leave without answers.

Luke used the Force to summon a staff and tried to force Rey back toward the *Falcon*.

Rey was ready for each strike. The harsh wastes of Jakku had taught her how to survive, and her keen connection to the Force helped her anticipate Luke's every move—so much so that she was able to knock Luke to the ground.

Luke realized there was only one way to ensure that Rey left forever. And that was to tell her the truth.

Luke told Rey he had sensed a darkness growing inside young Ben.

One night, as he checked on his sleeping nephew, he saw a flash of what Ben could become and instinctively grabbed his lightsaber. It was only a moment, and Luke quickly stopped himself from acting on what he had seen, but at that moment, Ben woke up and sensed Luke's intentions. Ben destroyed Luke's training temple and fled to Snoke's side.

Rey shook her head.

"You failed him by thinking his choice was made. It wasn't," said Rey. "He's our last hope."

Luke tried to convince her that it was too late. "This is not going to go the way you think."

But Rey was determined.

Luke watched as Rey, Chewie, and R2 boarded the *Falcon* and flew off into the vast reaches of space. Rey charted a course for the First Order's Mega-Destroyer. She trusted that the Force would lead her to Kylo so she could bring him back to the light.

It seemed like the Force was guiding Rose and Finn, too. They were in a fast, fully fueled ship, piloted by a man with exactly the skills they needed to infiltrate the First Order Mega-Destroyer and stop it from tracking the Resistance.

They just needed to convince DJ to help them. DJ didn't strike Rose as the kind of man who would do something because it was "the right thing to do." So instead, she offered him the thing he cared about most in the world: money.

Rose yanked off the valuable medallion from around her neck and tossed it to DJ as payment for his help.

The moment the *Falcon* disappeared from sight, Luke grabbed a torch and stumbled toward the cave with the tree. It had been foolish of him to keep the library there. If he really wanted the Jedi to end, their knowledge had to be wiped from the galaxy.

Luke held his torch near the tree, ready to act, when a bolt of lightning struck the tree. Flames coursed down its trunk and toward the hollow of the library.

Without thinking, Luke ran to protect the tree he had almost destroyed himself. Then he heard a voice.

"Heeded my words not did you, Young Skywalker." It was Yoda.
The sight of Luke's old teacher filled him with joy—and regret.

"'Pass on what you have learned,'" Yoda reminded him. "The greatest teacher failure is."

Luke knew Yoda was right. It was time for him to make a choice.

Rey could feel her connection to Kylo guiding her as she flew the *Falcon*. She stopped the ship just out of range of the Mega-Destroyer and hopped into an escape pod. She refused to drag Chewie and R2 into this situation, but she knew she had to try to save Kylo.

As soon as Rey's pod entered scanning range, a squadron of TIE fighters flanked it and escorted the pod into the Mega-Destroyer's hangar bay, where Kylo was waiting.

"When we touched, I saw your future," Rey said calmly. "You will turn."

"You're wrong," Kylo countered as he led her before Snoke. "When we touched, I saw your past. When the moment comes, you'll be the one to turn." He paused. "I know who your parents are."

Kylo presented her to his master.

"Well done, my good and faithful apprentice," Snoke said. "My faith in you is restored."

In another wing of the Mega-Destroyer, DJ had held up his end of the bargain. He had cracked the First Order clearance codes and snuck Rose, Finn, and BB-8 on board. They had disguised themselves as First Order officers and were making their way through the ship to get to the transmitter.

Finn remembered every twist and turn of the ship's corridors. If anyone could get them there safely, it was him.

But back with the Resistance fleet, Poe was growing impatient. Holdo still refused to tell Poe her plan, but he knew Finn and Rose were close to disabling the Mega-Destroyer's tracker. Poe decided it was time to take matters into his own hands.

He and a few other Resistance crew members decided to stand up to Holdo. "I'm relieving you of duty," Poe said, blaster drawn. It was a mutiny!

On board the Mega-Destroyer, Snoke took Rey's lightsaber from her and examined the powerful weapon. Rey hated to see his disgusting hands touching her weapon. She called out to Kylo, begging him to help her.

Snoke laughed. He revealed that *he* was the one who had bridged Rey and Kylo's minds. Their bond wasn't destiny. It was all according to Snoke's plan. "For you, all is lost," Snoke told Rey with a cruel smile.

Not far off, Rose, Finn, and DJ had almost reached the tracking device.

"It's right through—" Finn began, but then stopped when he saw the platoon of stormtroopers ahead of them.

The white-armored soldiers were commanded by Finn's former leader, Captain Phasma.

DJ waved to Rose and Finn, then went to join Phasma and the stormtroopers.

DJ had betrayed them!

Rose wondered if he had been working for the First Order the entire time. It was impossible to know. But Phasma had clearly made DJ a better offer than an old medallion.

Poe had no idea his friends were in such grave danger. He was busy trying to keep control of the bridge. Poe had sealed off the command center, locking himself and Holdo inside. He could hear Holdo's allies banging at the door. Poe told himself he just needed to buy Rose and Finn enough time to deactivate the tracking device.

But the bridge door suddenly burst open to reveal—General Leia! She had recovered in the medbay and was ready to take command again.

Leia ordered everyone to carry on with Holdo's original plan: the Resistance members would evacuate the main Resistance cruiser in transports launched into space as the cruiser continued on its original course.

"For the transports to escape, someone has to stay behind and pilot the cruiser," Holdo said.

Leia feared she knew what her old friend was saying.

"I'm afraid I outrank you, Princess," Holdo continued. "And an admiral goes down with her ship."

Leia shook her friend's hand and said good-bye.

Leia explained Holdo's strategy as the transports took off.

"There are still a few shadow planets in deep space," said Leia. "During the days of the Rebellion, we'd use them as hideouts."

They were going to land on a nearby shadow planet named Crait where they could signal for help. Meanwhile, Holdo would distract the First Order for as long as possible.

Leia hoped that Poe now understood what made a hero—not flashy flying and death-defying odds, but thoughtful sacrifice. She needed him to learn that so he could be a good leader.

But with the First Order firing on the Resistance transports, Poe wondered if he'd ever have a chance to become the leader Leia hoped for.

Back on the Mega-Destroyer, Snoke was still tormenting Rey.
But what neither Snoke nor Rey noticed was that Kylo had a plan of his own.
While Snoke was distracted, Kylo used the Force to silently turn Luke's
lightsaber so it faced Snoke.

In one swift movement, Kylo ignited the weapon, destroying Snoke forever.
    Rey was overjoyed. Kylo had joined her—just as she had foreseen.
Together they could return to Luke and rebuild the Jedi Order. None of them
would be alone anymore.
    But there was no time to celebrate.

Snoke's deadly Praetorian Guard descended on Rey and Kylo.

Rey and Kylo battled the guards, but the red-armored team of elite troopers was extremely skilled and almost impossible to overpower.

Only by working together, as a perfect team, were Rey and Kylo able to defeat them.

Once they were safe, Rey turned breathlessly to Kylo.

"I knew there was good in you," she said.

But Kylo's face hardened. Something was wrong.

Nearby, Phasma's stormtroopers pushed Rose and Finn to the ground and bound their hands. She was ready to put an end to the Resistance fighters.

"Blasters are too good for them," Phasma said. "Let's make it hurt."

Finn heard a familiar buzz and saw two executioner troopers readying their laser axes.

Finn and Rose searched desperately for a way to escape. They couldn't let Phasma stop them now.

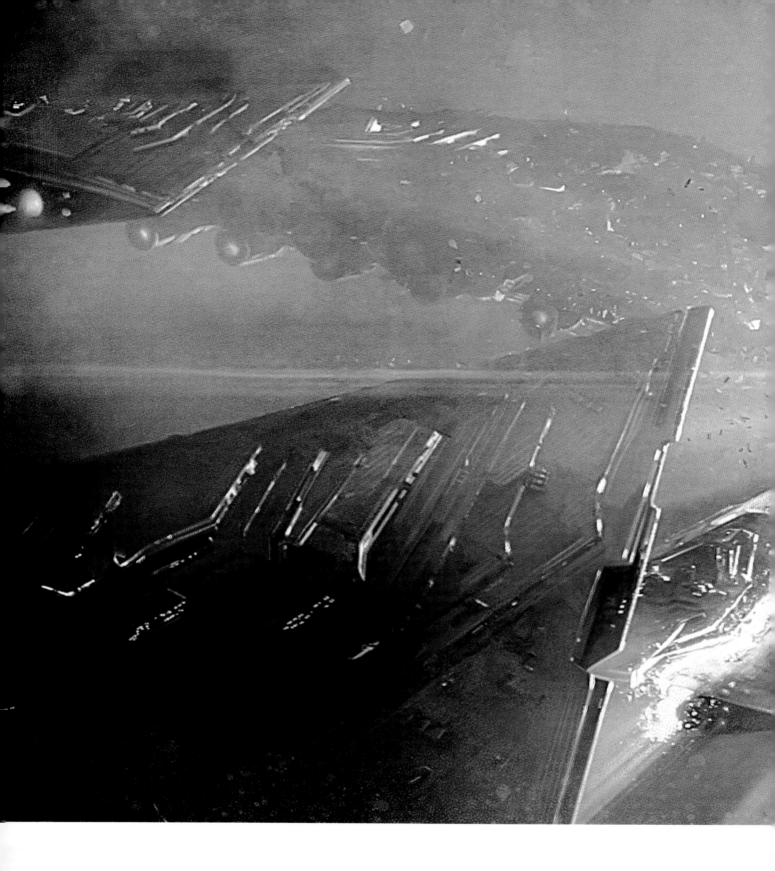

The Resistance needed to be saved. The First Order was still taking out the transports, and soon there wouldn't be any Resistance members left. Alone on the main Resistance cruiser, Holdo knew what she had to do.

Holdo set coordinates to jump the ship to hyperspace . . . *through* the First Order's Mega-Destroyer!

Back in Snoke's chambers, Kylo and Rey circled each other.

Kylo had no intention of turning to the light side. Instead, he urged Rey to join him, to rule the galaxy by his side. When Rey refused, he tried to take her lightsaber. Rey focused all her strength on drawing the weapon back to her. Kylo did the same.

The lightsaber trembled in midair between them as both Kylo and Rey fought to possess the blade.

"You know the truth about your parents," Kylo snarled. "Say it!"

And in that moment, she knew the answer she had both longed for and feared her whole life.

"They were nobody."

Overwhelmed by the power flowing through it, the lightsaber split in two, just as Holdo's ship tore through the Mega-Destroyer.

BB-8 used the same moment to start firing on the troopers who had captured Finn and Rose—from a giant two-legged walker!

The ensuing chaos allowed Rose and Finn to free themselves.

The clever droid had saved them once again.

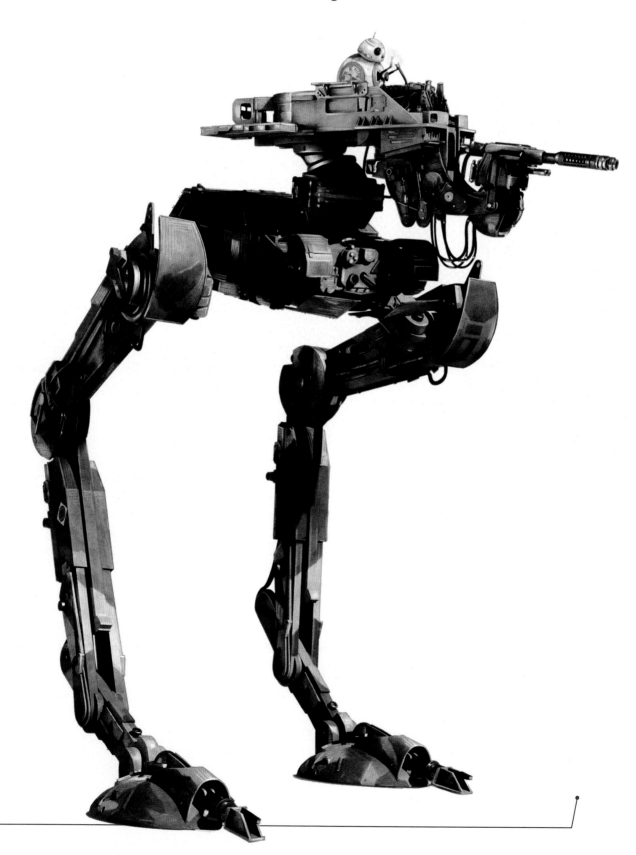

But Captain Phasma was still standing.

Finn grabbed a riot baton from one of the fallen stormtroopers and prepared to fight. He could feel the fury radiating from her. Finn and his Resistance friends had humiliated her twice. And she wanted revenge.

"You were always scum," she spat.

"Rebel scum," Finn replied proudly.

Finn's blade sparked against Phasma's weapon as they connected. She matched him blow for blow. After all, Phasma had trained Finn to be a soldier. But he had learned a few tricks since leaving the First Order. Finn slammed his baton down into Phasma's mask, cracking her chrome helmet. He saw fear flash in Phasma's blue eye before she was knocked unconscious.

With the Mega-Destroyer crumbling around her, Rey fled for an escape pod just as General Hux entered Snoke's chambers.

Kylo was quick to blame their former leader's death on Rey. General Hux was not one to question a powerful Force user with a lightsaber.

Hux bowed his head toward Kylo. "Supreme Leader."

Now Kylo was in control of the entire First Order.

With Phasma defeated, Rose, Finn, and BB-8 stole a First Order light shuttle and headed for Crait to meet up with the rest of the Resistance.

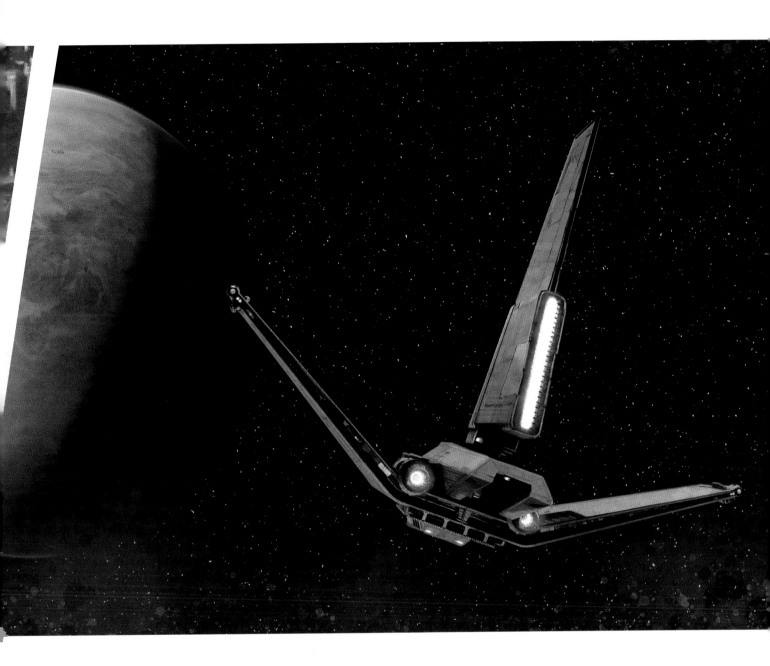

There the Resistance forces had barricaded themselves in an old Rebellion base. The base hadn't been used in years, and many areas had been taken over by the strange crystal foxes that lived on the planet.

The ships stored at the base were old, but they could still fly.

The Resistance would make its last stand against the First Order on Crait and send out desperate pleas for help from its allies.

When Rose and Finn arrived at the Resistance base, Leia and Poe saw their stolen First Order ship and began firing at them. They thought the ship had come to attack!

"Don't shoot!" Finn cried. "It's us!"

He and Rose peeked out of the ship.

Leia and Poe were relieved to see them.

The Rebellion base was protected by a giant fortified door. But that door was also the only way in or out, trapping them inside the mountainous shelter. As Rose, Finn, and the Resistance pilots ran to their ships, the First Order was priming their battering ram cannon. The Resistance fighters needed to destroy it before it destroyed the only thing separating them from their enemies.

Poe, Finn, Rose, and a few other Resistance members hopped into a squadron of old ski speeders and flew out to fight the First Order.

In the cockpit of his ski speeder, Finn took a deep breath as he headed toward the attacking First Order army. He had faced death more than once that day, and he was glad to have his friends by his side.

As wave after wave of First Order AT-AT walkers and TIE fighters attacked, it was clear the Resistance was completely outnumbered.

Finn looked to the horizon and felt a glimmer of hope for the first time since he had arrived on Crait.

The unmistakable shape of the *Millennium Falcon* was flying toward them, and on board Rey, Chewie, and R2 were ready to help.

While Chewie flew the ship, Rey hopped into the gunner seat and began firing on TIE fighters.

"Chewie!" Rey yelled into her headset. "Peel off from the battle! Draw them away from the speeders!"

The *Millennium Falcon* led away the entire squadron of TIEs. Finn cheered as the ships disappeared in the distance. But the battering ram was almost ready to fire.

Finn knew the door wouldn't last much longer against such a powerful force. He had to stop it. So Finn set his ski speeder on a crash course with the battering ram.

Rose saw what Finn was doing and called out to him to stop. She promised him that they would find another way to beat the First Order. It wasn't worth Finn's life. When Finn refused to listen, Rose ran her ski speeder into the side of Finn's, causing both to crash.

Finn climbed out of his broken craft and ran to Rose's side.

"Why did you stop me?" he asked.

Rose kissed him in reply. As she did, a blast from the First Order battering ram struck the Rebellion base's door.

Leia prepared to surrender.

"We fought to the end. But the galaxy has lost its hope. The spark is out."

Then she heard footsteps in the hallway behind her. Before she could even turn around, she knew who it was.

"Luke," she breathed.

The old Jedi searched for the right words to say. "Leia. I'm sorry."

When the Resistance needed him most, Luke Skywalker answered the call.
He stood in the doorway of the Rebellion base and prepared to fight.
Kylo could barely believe his eyes when he saw Luke facing him on the
battlefield. He was stunned for a moment as memories of his old mentor
threatened to overwhelm him. Then Kylo snapped back to the present.

"Fire everything we have!" he screamed.

Blast after blast landed in the doorway where Luke stood, until a haze of smoke covered the area. Kylo held his breath and waited for it to clear. But when the smoke parted, Kylo saw Luke still standing tall, untouched by the attack.

The only way Kylo was going to defeat Luke was if he did it
himself. He left his ship and prepared to fight his former teacher
face to face.

Luke silently raised his own blade and prepared for Kylo's attack.

The push and pull of Kylo and Luke's battle felt familiar to both master and apprentice.

"Strike me down in anger, and I'll always be with you," Luke said. "Just like your father."

Kylo was done being lectured by Luke, or any other master.
"The Resistance is dead. The war is over." Kylo seethed.
Luke disagreed. "The Rebellion is reborn today. The war is just beginning. And I will not be the last Jedi."

As Luke and Kylo fought, the Resistance had the distraction it needed to regroup inside the Rebellion base, but there was no way to escape.

Then Poe saw the crystal foxes darting through the cave.

"Follow me," Poe said.

Everyone turned to General Organa as if waiting for an order. "What are you looking at me for? Follow him," she said.

She stepped behind Poe, the first to follow his instructions.

Poe and the rest of the Resistance followed the foxes down one of the tunnels, deeper and deeper into the mountain. They saw a glimmer of light ahead. It was a way out!

But then they realized that the hole in the rocks was far too small for anything other than a fox to crawl through.

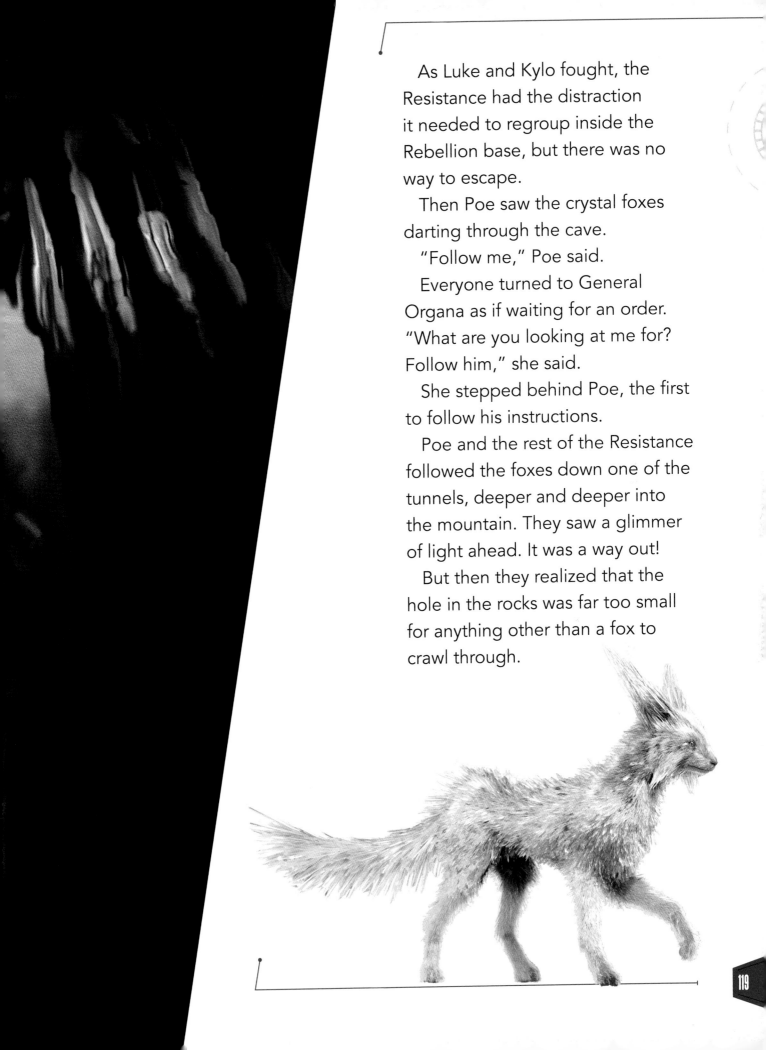

Meanwhile, Rey had sensed that her friends needed her help.

She had Chewbacca fly the *Falcon* in low over the mountains.

"They've gotta be somewhere. Keep scanning for life-forms!"

The Force led Rey to the small opening in the rocks that Poe and the Resistance had found from within. The gap was small, and the mountain was huge. But Rey knew she had to try.

Rey quieted her mind and reached out with the Force. The passage began to tremble as Rey lifted massive rocks up and away from the tunnel, clearing the opening.

Luke sensed that the Resistance had made it to safety. He immediately stopped fighting and dropped his lightsaber gently at his side.

Kylo brought the full force of his lightsaber down on Luke—but the blade passed through the old Jedi without leaving a mark.

"See you around, kid," Luke said.
Then he started to disappear.

Back on Ahch-To, Luke faded away on the meditation ledge, becoming one with the Force.

It had taken everything he had to project so much of himself onto Crait. Drawing that much power directly from the Force had consequences. But Luke was happy to pay them. His final act had saved Leia, Rey, and the Resistance.

The Jedi would continue, even though Luke would be gone.

The surviving members of the Resistance crowded onto the *Millennium Falcon*, and the ship fled to the safety of hyperspace.

The journey ahead would be difficult. All that remained of the Resistance fit on a single ship. And Rey sensed that Luke was gone.

But an important piece of Luke's legacy survived: the Jedi texts. Rey had snuck them on board the *Falcon* before leaving Ahch-To, hoping they would have the information she needed to continue her training as a Jedi.

Rey searched for Leia. She wanted to tell her about Luke's last moments.

"I felt it," Rey said. "But it wasn't sadness or pain. It was peace. And purpose."

"I felt it, too," Leia said.

Rey should have known. Leia always seemed to know the right thing to say. Rey had wanted to comfort Leia, but she found she was the one who needed comforting.

"Kylo is stronger than ever," Rey said. "He has an army and an iron grip on the galaxy. How do we build a rebellion from this?"

But Leia gestured around at all their Resistance friends.

"We have everything we need," Leia said.